THE LEGEND OF LA LLORONA

THE LEGEND OF LA LLORONA

Rudolfo A. Anaya

a short novel

TONATIUH–QUINTO SOL INTERNATIONAL, INC.
Publishers
Post Office Box 9275
Berkeley, California 94709 USA

Library of Congress Catalogue Card Number: 84-51750

ISBN: 0-89229-015-3

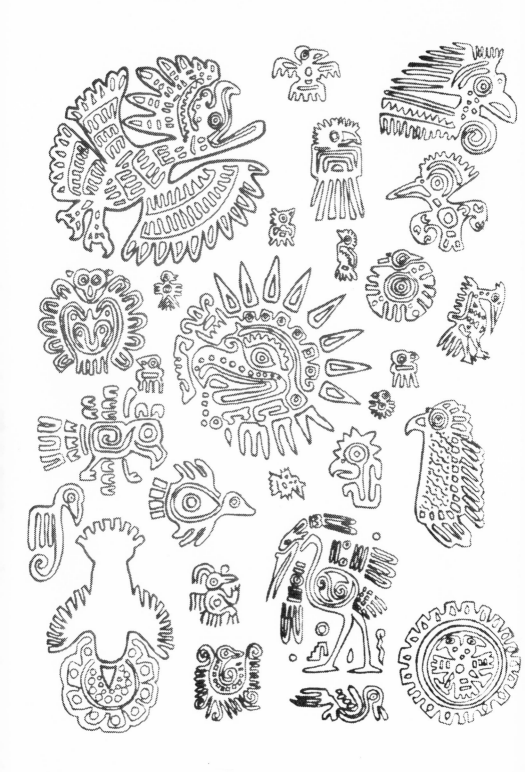

Contents

A NEW TIME

MALINTZIN

THE CAPTAIN

A PLEDGE OF LOVE

MARCH TO MEXICO

MOCTEZUMA

THE CHILDREN

THE LAKE

A PRINCESS

THE WAR GOD

ATTEMPT TO ESCAPE

BETRAYAL

THE SACRIFICE

LA LLORONA

A NEW TIME

It was the year One-Reed according to the Aztec Calendar of the Sun, an era had come to an end. Now the people of Mexico-Tenochtitlan made preparations to celebrate the momentous event: the end of a fifty-two year cycle on their sacred calendar. Ominous signs filled the air, and the Aztec people went about their business in a solemn and apprehensive mood.

The sun and planets and stars were carefully observed by the priests of the temples. The old cycle of time was dying, and a new era would be ushered in. The priests would ascend the great Pyramid of the Sun at Teotihuacan, the center of worship for the Aztecs of Tenochtitlan, and there they would offer sacrifices to the Sun God. Captives of war and maidens taken from the enemy villages would be sacrificed to restore the power of the dying sun.

For one dread-filled day and night all the fires of Tenochtitlan would be extinguished, the marvelous city of the Aztecs would be without light. A silence would descend upon the people, dread would fill their hearts. And finally when the sacrifices were complete, all would await a signal from the priests. If the Sun God accepted the sacrifices of the priests, the sun would shine brightly, the new cycle of time would begin. Then the priests would stir the embers of the old fire, the new, sacred fire would be rekindled and these new coals would be carried by runners to the hearths of the people of Tenochtitlan.

However, it was not only the end of an era which preoccupied the Aztecs in that fateful year of 1516; there was something more ominous in the air. At the root of the Aztec soul there was a legend whose prophecy filled the people with doubts and fears and anxious expectations. According to the legend, this was the year the god Quetzalcoatl was destined to return from his exile in the east. Quetzalcoatl, the plumed serpent, god of wisdom and culture, Lord of Light, this was his time to return! He who was both morning star and brother of the sun, he would return! This the legend foretold, the god Quetzalcoatl would return to his people!

This wise and noble god had sown the seeds of the Aztec civilization, his guiding hand had brought glory and pride to the wandering Aztecs. The marvelous city of Tenochtitlan and all its temples and pyramids were built to honor the Lord of Light and the other gods of the Aztecs. Then another god rose to prominence, the god of the Aztec warriors, Huitzilopochtli, the God of War. Huitzilopochtli grew strong, and those who honored him made him the dominant god of Tenochtitlan, and they exiled the God of Light, Quetzalcoatl. But Quetzalcoatl had vowed to return to rule his people, and now was the time of his return.

Would he return with a smile in his heart, or with a frown on his brow? Would his footsteps shake the earth as the thunder of the summer storms shook the mountains? Would he do battle with the God of War and in their struggle bring down the heavens? Would dark night fill the cosmos if this god who was the Morning Star moved from the skies to return to earth? These and many other questions filled the people of Tenochtitlan with dread and anxiety.

The same questions disturbed Moctezuma, the king and priest-god of the Aztecs, as he walked somberly in the gardens of his palace. For many days he did not eat, and he took no drink. His attendants were greatly concerned as they watched their lord pace the luxurious garden where the jacarandas grew and the fragrance of sweet jasmine filled the night air. On the shoulders of their lord rested the fate of their far-flung empire. If Quetzalcoatl returned, it was Moctezuma who would welcome the god and speak to him.

In the marketplace of the city, the people whispered and waited. In the temples the priests grew apprehensive and fearful. It was the ancestors of the priests who had cast the god Quetzalcoatl into exile, and now he was returning. What would he say to the priests?

The brave Aztec warriors who knew no fear in battle and who had conquered many neighboring tribes, these soldiers of the God of War now felt fear enter their hearts. Chanting the war songs of Huitzilopochtli they had overcome their enemies, they had brought the treasures of the land to Tenochtitlan, and they had brought many captives to build the temples to their gods. During the ritual War of Flowers they had taken many warriors captive, brave men who were sacrificed at the temples. They had conquered the surrounding native villages and demanded yearly tribute, wealth which ennobled the dazzling city of Tenochtitlan. But now a god who was stronger and wiser than the God of War was returning to rule over the people of Tenochtitlan. The God of War,

Huitzilopochtli, would be swept aside, and this
is why terror and weakness filled their hearts.

The people of the city spoke softly as they
went about their daily chores. If Quetzalcoatl
came in anger, he would bring tempests of wind,
fire and thunder which would destroy their beloved city. Death would stalk the streets. This
was the foreboding which filled the city, touching
everyone, even the children. Everyone feared the
prophecy would be fulfilled, the end of an era
was eminent.

During this time other disquieting news was
brought by messengers from eastern coasts. The
news was delivered directly to Moctezuma and his
priests, and it was whispered to the people. When
the people met in the marketplace they discussed
the strange rumors they had heard. On the gentle
waters of the eastern sea, it was said, strange
and incredible sights were observed. Houses with
sails were seen upon the sea.

And the reports grew more strange and fantastic.
These houses were the abode of the priests of
Quetzalcoatl, it was reported, and priests with
pale skins who wore the feathers of their god on
their faces had been seen on these sailing houses.

It is true, the vendors of the marketplace
whispered. The first messengers of the Sun God
have come from the east where the sun rises. They
speak a strange tongue, they are pale even as the
Lord of Light Quetzalcoatl, and on their faces
grow the feathers of the god.

Ay, Lord of Life, now the end of our way of life
is near! Now the arrival of the god Quetzalcoatl
is imminent!

MALINTZIN

Yes, it was true, the strangers from across the wide waters had arrived. In 1516 a Spanish ship exploring the eastern coast of Mexico was shipwrecked, and a few survivors were cast upon the white beach. There they were found by the natives of the region. Naked and shivering from their ordeal, they were rescued by the natives who gave them food and clothes.

These Spanish soldiers quickly learned the native ways. They had found paradise, they thought. Here the climate was mild, food was plentiful, and they feasted on fish from the coastal waters and tropical fruits they had never before tasted. The natives were healthy and content and appeared to live in peace.

Life with the people of the coast was pleasant, but the soldiers were not content. They knew that soon other ships would come and they would be rescued. After all, they had come to make their fortunes in the New World, not to idle their time away. So each day the soldiers went to the beach where they sat and gazed at the sea, waiting for the ships they were sure would come.

Some of the natives of the village went with them, and they too sat and gazed at the waters of the wide gulf.

"We wait for our Captain," the soldiers said. "He will come."

The natives nodded and murmured among themselves. These, they believed, were the first messengers of the Aztec God, Quetzalcoatl. They waited for their god. Messengers were sent inland, to the great capital city of Tenochtitlan, to the priest-god Moctezuma. The first priests of Quetzalcoatl have arrived, the messages said, and now they await the arrival of their god. These were the messages which caused so much rumor and worry in Mexico-Tenochtitlan.

One young woman of the coastal village did not believe that the poor, bedraggled soldiers she helped pull from the sea were the messengers of the gods. This woman was Malintzin, daughter of the chief of the village. She had looked closely at the soldiers when they lay on the beach, coughing and gasping for air. These are not priests or gods, she thought, these are men.

The naked soldiers had shivered with cold. Hair covered their faces, chests, arms and legs. They are covered with hair, she thought, but they are still men. Later she laughed when her people said the sailors were covered with feathers.

It was Malintzin's eighteenth summer, and she was considered a woman, but she had not yet married. In her village Malintzin was believed to have great powers. It was not only her height and striking beauty which distinguished her from other girls her age who were already taking husbands and starting families, no, it was more. Malintzin was the daughter of the chief. Because she was not married she was allowed to sit with the village council when it discussed the social ceremonies of the village. Before her eighteenth summer she

had already argued before the council that the
village should not be dominated by the Aztec empire
and tribute should not be sent to Moctezuma. The
argument continued among the tribes of the coastal
region, whether to be independent and constantly
face the wrath of the giant Aztec federation, or
to join the Aztecs as a tributary state. When
messengers were sent to Moctezuma telling of the
strangers and their houses which sailed upon the
water, she argued that the report should state
that pale men were found, not the priests of
Quetzalcoatl.

But there was more to this young woman of oval
face and high cheek bones. At the time of Malintzin's birth the village priest read the signs
of the planets, and it was foretold that the baby
Malintzin would live to be a legend in the time
of the new era. At an early age she was sent to
study with the priests and the village shaman.
Her powers were exceptional. Flames sputtered
and died or rose into lively dance when she walked
by, obeying her wish, because fire was the element
of her ascending sign. Even the unclean waters
of the swamps grew clean at her touch, and later
when she had learned all the remedies of the shaman
she cured many illnesses with water and herbs.

Even before her puberty she visited many
neighboring villages with her shaman, and she
learned the customs and languages of the coastal
people. She was like a bird who learns to imitate
the songs of other birds. When the Aztec tax
collectors came to her village she learned enough
of their language to converse with them. After
the shipwrecked Spanish soldiers had been in her
village a few months, she was soon speaking their
language.

She was truly a gifted woman, a noble person,
and full of kindness when she went to heal the
old and the infirm. An aura of light seemed to
glow around her. On her eleventh summer when she

became a woman and was given her name, Malintzin, she was dressed in a cotton skirt of white, with a huipil of many colors. She had worn white since that time.

The young men of the village admired her beauty and smiled at her when she passed by, but Malintzin remained aloof. The Aztec prophecy had affected the life of her village, and according to it a new era was about to dawn. Malintzin had decided to wait and see what this new age delivered to her.

THE CAPTAIN

At last the long awaited Spanish ships arrived. One clear day they were sighted on the rolling waters of the gulf. Messengers ran from village to village on the coast, and quickly the people gathered. The Spanish soldiers lit fires and burned green leaves from the palm trees, so a column of smoke filled the air. There was shouting and excitement as the natives gathered to watch the houses which floated on the water and which now lay bobbing on the sea. The natives were filled with excitement and apprehension. Had Quetzalcoatl returned? Expectancy filled the air.

For a long time they waited, then smaller boats left the ships and came toward the shore. Men who looked like the first shipwrecked Spaniards were in the boats.

"We're saved!" the soldiers on the beach cried. "We're saved!" There was great rejoicing as the two groups met. They embraced each other, they cried openly.

The natives watched in awe. There were many of these messengers of the god. Men of Iron, they called them later when they had touched their steel helmets and breastplates. Men of light colored eyes. Plumed men on whose faces grew thick beards. Men of a foreign tongue. Were these the messengers and priests of Quetzalcoatl?

The village chiefs gathered to greet the Spanish soldiers. In peace they greeted them. Then they brought Malintzin forward, to interpret for them because she knew their language. Now the man they had all waited for, the man they called the Captain, arrived. He stepped forward and looked at Malintzin.

A heathen who can speak the language of Castile, the Captain thought. What a beautiful creature. He took her hand and felt Malintzin's strength. Then he smiled.

"What is your name?" he asked.

"I am Malintzin," she replied.

"Malinche," he repeated the name, changing the sound, assuring she would thereafter be known as Malinche.

"Tell your people we come in peace," he told her, and she interpreted the message. The natives nodded in approval.

Then the Captain looked around and claimed the land for His Majesty, the King. The soldiers cheered. The Spanish friars set up a crude altar on the beach and said mass. The Indians watched closely. There on the altar was the tree of life, a sacred symbol, the Cross of Christ.

Then the horses were brought from the ships, and the soldiers mounted them and rode back and forth on the beach. The natives again grew apprehensive when they saw these large, strange animals. Later the soldiers fired their harquebuses, the matchlock muskets, and the air was filled with thunder and the sharp smoke of burned gunpowder. The natives ran in fear. A new age had indeed dawned on the shores of the New World.

The following day the soldiers from the boats marched up the beach to another village, and there they encountered an ambush. The natives attacked with arrows, stones from slings, and axes with obsidian lined edges. For a short time the Spaniards were surprised and fell back. Then they responded with the deadly fire of their muskets and cannon. The earth seemed to shake, acrid smoke filled the green jungle. The soldiers on horseback attacked, using their horses to run down the native warriors. They slashed with their swords and soon the ground was red with blood. The terrified natives withdrew, no match for the new kind of warfare which had come to their land. The military might of the Spaniard was tested and proved superior. These messengers from Quetzalcoatl were invincible.

The soldiers soon heard rumors from the natives about the rich and mighty city of Tenochtitlan far to the west. There, they had heard, the streets were paved with gold and even ordinary household objects were studded with precious stones. The Captain vowed to conquer this great city.

The various native groups along the coast were in a quandry. Some continued to resist the Spaniards, but some formed an alliance with them hoping to throw off the yoke of the Aztecs. They were tired of sending tribute to Moctezuma's empire. The Captain assured them that if they joined him they could march together against the Aztec rulers and free themselves. The people of the villages along the coast agreed.

A PLEDGE OF LOVE

During this time Malinche observed the Captain closely. Because she understood his language, he asked her to be at his side when he was engaged in negotiations with the natives. She agreed because the elders of her village had cast their lot with the Captain and his soldiers. But there was another reason for the decision. Since their first meeting she had felt much admiration and affection for the Captain. She felt excited when she saw him, delighted when she heard his voice. She was falling in love with the Captain, she was binding her life to his.

It was a natural thing to happen. He was a strong and brave warrior, a fearless soldier. He had turned back the warriors of other villages who had always threatened the peace of her people, and he was wise enough to make peace when he could. He was a handsome man. His eyes glowed and he smiled when he saw Malinche. He too was falling in love with the lovely interpreter who went with him everywhere. Only one thing remained between them. The Captain and his friars

insisted that the natives give up their own reli-
gious ceremonies and take the religion of their
god.   Christ, not Quetzalcoatl, was their divine
inspiration.

One evening, on the night before the march to
Tenochtitlan was to begin, the Captain sought out
Malinche.   He found her at the village temple.
A frown crossed his face, but he waited patiently.
When she arose she greeted him.

"Good evening, my Captain," she said.

"Malinche," he said, "come walk with me.   There
is something very important I must tell you."

The night was alive with the chirp of night
crickets and the occasional calls of jungle birds.
Overhead the sky was clear, the stars shone with
a bright glitter.   In their huts the people prepared the evening meal, and the air was sweet with
the aroma of fresh baked fish, vegetables, and
corn tortillas.   Children played joyfully.   All
greeted Malinche and the Captain as they strolled
in the jasmine fragrant night.

"A pleasant sight," the Captain mused.

"Even for a soldier?" Malinche asked.

"Ah, yes, we know as well, or better than most,
the comfort of a quiet home, the joy of children.
Someday it may be that all my soldiers settle in
this land, to marry and raise families.   But for
now there is something more important on my mind.
Soon we begin our journey to Mexico-Tenochtitlan."

Here the Captain paused.   He turned and looked
at Malinche.   In the moonlight her face shone
with beauty.   He resisted the impulse to touch
her, to hold her in his arms and reveal his real
feelings.

"I want you to come with us," he said.

"As your interpreter?" Malinche asked.

"Yes."

"I am ready to serve you, my Captain," Malinche
said.   While the quick answer surprised the Captain,
it surprised Malinche even more.   She knew the

soldiers were leaving, and she had felt a sadness
because it meant the Captain would be gone. She
had even thought vaguely about going with them,
but she hadn't realized that her decision would
come so quickly once he asked. Yes, this was
love, she thought. She was truly ready to serve
this warrior.

"You will go?" the Captain said.

"Yes."

"Wonderful!" he exclaimed. "What good news!"
He reached out and hugged her. The children
playing nearby stopped their game to watch. Their
warriors did not hug women in public. And to them
Malinche had the status of a goddess! What could
this mean? What fruit would this alliance bear?

"My Captain," Malinche smiled. He looked at
the children.

"I beg your pardon," the Captain bowed. "It's
that I'm overjoyed with the news. You will be
our most valuable asset. And you know that all
my soldiers love and respect you. Their morale
will be increased a hundredfold when I tell them
the news."

"And yours, my Captain?" Malinche asked.

"You know how I feel," he replied.

"I know you value my ability as an interpreter,"
she smiled.

"It is more than that," he said and looked
closely at her. "Since the day I met you, I
have respected and honored you. And now you
know I love you." He paused, afraid he had gone
too far with this noble woman whom the villagers
revered as a goddess.

"As you profess your love for me, so I give
mine to you," Malinche told him. "Love has conquered my heart. I will follow you wherever you go."

The Captain gazed softly at Malinche. He touched
her cheek then kissed her lightly on the forehead.
"I will respect your love and never dishonor it.
You will be my equal partner in this adventure
which awaits us."

Malinche smiled.   Now the happiness she had kept
in check flooded her being and made her body tingle
with excitement.   The Aztec prophecy had brought
this man to unite with her.   She would give up
her home and family to follow him.   Such a strong
emotion was her love, she would give up everything
to go with this warrior who had come from the
land of the sun.   So, she thought as she stood
with him in the perfume of the sweet night and
felt his arm around her, so this is what the prophecy
at my birth meant.   That I should give my love
to this man, and bear his children.

Malinche watched as the Captain consolidated
his forces in the towns of the eastern coast.
With soothing and flattering words he made old
enemies join together to oppose the Aztec might,
all the while sending word to Moctezuma that he
was a friend.   The allies of the Captain grew,
and Moctezuma was worried.   He sent the Captain
gifts of gold and told him to stay away from
Tenochtitlan, because now the military might of
the Spaniards was known and feared.   Messengers
had already carried the news to Moctezuma that
these men from the east were gods and that their
cannon and musket fire was deadly.   And these
gods made war while riding huge beasts bigger
than deer.   The fame of the Captain and his men
spread.

But there was rebellion within the Captain's
ranks.   Some of his men wanted to return to
their homes in Cuba, some wanted to report to
the Governor that the Captain was a dangerous
man.   The Captain talked to these men, gave them
gifts of gold, persuaded them to march with him
to Mexico-Tenochtitlan.   They would all be rich
men, he told them.   Then they would return to
Cuba and give the Governor an accounting of
everything, and they would give this same report
to Don Carlos, His Majesty the King of Spain.
Some of the men did not agree, and to prevent

their escape the Captain ordered that the ships
should be stripped and burned.   With the ships destroyed there was no turning back.   All would have
to join in the march to Mexico, but not all would
live to see the grandeur of that city and the noble,
magnificent ruler, Moctezuma.

MARCH TO MEXICO

The great march inland to Mexico-Tenochtitlan began. Everywhere the Captain went he made allies of the old enemies of the Aztecs. Some of these natives of the provinces were tired of paying taxes to the Aztecs, and they were tired of having to supply their women and daughters as sacrificial victims to the Aztec gods. Those natives who did not join the Spanish cause were subdued with force.

And everywhere he went the Captain destroyed the old gods of the people. He stripped the temples bare and his friars erected crosses on top of them. The conquest was a ruthless affair, the people were divided and conquered.

It saddened Malinche to see the temples destroyed. True, she had accepted the Christian teachings of love and mercy, but she had not forgotten the ways of her people.

"Why must you destroy the temples?" she asked the Captain.

"To destroy the will of the people you must destroy what they believe," he said. "We believe in only one God, not in heathen idols."

Malinche went away saddened. She saw too much destruction in their path to take any pleasure in the wonders of the march. And wonders there were. They met new people. They climbed mountains where the air was cool and thin. In front of them rose the sacred and ancient volcanoes of Cholula, Popocatepetl, the male mountain, and leagues away at his side, Iztaccihuatl, the female mountain.

From the shaman of Cholula, Malinche learned the legend of the mountains.

"The male mountain was once a warrior," the old man said. "He fell in love with a maiden from this village. But he was from another people, and her father would not allow the marriage. She grew sad and died. The warrior came and burned incense at her funeral, and the smoke rose to take the shape of the female mountain. Then the warrior rose in anger and told the gods he would remain with her forever. There where he stood the male mountain was born, an angry volcano who can still be heard singing his song of love for the woman. They are together."

Malinche understood the story. It was a story of love, preserved in the legends of the people. What she couldn't understand was the war that took place a few days later. Unprovoked, the Captain and his soldiers fell upon the people of Cholula and killed hundreds. It was a slaughter which sent waves of fear throughout the provinces. It made Malinche's heart cold and hard. The warriors she had trusted and respected were capable of the most inhumane acts.

How, she wondered, can I keep my love for the Captain when he rises so cruelly against my people. Again, she sought out the shaman, as was her custom wherever she went.

"We cannot speak of love now," the old man said. "Our hearts are filled with grief as we bury

our dead. Our hearts are cold with fear. Your love
has bound you to the man known as the Captain of
this cruel army. Now you must stay at his side.
You are fixed to his side, even as the female mountain is fixed to the male mountain."

He said this and placed his hand on Malinche's
stomach. "His sons grow in you."

Malinche pulled back in shock. Even she had
not yet felt the pregnancy the old man announced.
Was it possible?

"Yes," he said, as if he had read her mind.
"You will give birth to twin sons. One will be as
the War God and follow the steps of the warrior.
The other will be as the God of Peace, and sing of
peace. You will be in the city of the Aztecs when
they are born, and you must go to the priests of
the temple and raise your sons in the way of the
Aztec. This is your destiny." Then he turned
and quickly hurried away, leaving Malinche to muse
over the grave words the shaman had spoken, yet
happy with the news that she was carrying twin
sons.

What the old man said was true. In the next
few days as they continued their march into Mexico
City she felt a change within her. She grew
weary often and had to pause to rest. When the
Captain heard the news, he was happy and ordered
a great feast to be held. The soldiers sang and
told stories around the campfires. Everyone was
happy.

Why shouldn't they be happy? The great capital
of the Aztecs was in sight. Mexico-Tenochtitlan
was just ahead. Messengers from Moctezuma came
daily now, appealing to the Captain not to come to
the city. And the Captain sent back glowing
messages saying he was coming in peace.

The following day Malinche went to the temple
to give thanks. She ordered the priests to sacrifice fowls and burn incense, but the Captain
found her and became angry.

"You are not to pray to heathen idols!" he shouted, and he ordered that all the statues which represented her gods should be smashed. The temple was cleared out and a cross placed on top. Malinche never again prayed to her gods in public, but still she carried them in her heart.

MOCTEZUMA

The arrival of the Spaniards in Mexico-Tenochtitlan was a momentous affair. When the soldiers stood on the hills surrounding the city they couldn't believe their eyes. All of the towns they had seen thus far were plain and simple, but here was a magnificent city which glittered in the sun.

The city lay in the valley of Mexico, surrounded by mountains, well protected from harsh weather and from roving enemies. In this valley of Anahuac there was a huge lake, and in the middle of the lake the city had been built on an island. Three causeways connected the city with the land. These causeways had bridges over them which could be lifted to allow the boats of the lake to pass or to keep enemies out. The rooftops were flat, and the ladders too could be lifted to make the houses inaccessible. It would be a difficult city to capture.

But Moctezuma had relented and invited the Spaniards to enter the city. Dignitaries came out to greet the soldiers, and they were led into the city. What marvelous things they saw! Whitewashed houses shone in the sun, clean and straight streets led to a grand central marketplace where the people met daily to do their business. Huge temples rose up into the sky. Not even in their native country had the soldiers seen such marvels.

Officials arrived with gifts, gold and carved works of gold, jade, precious feathers and cotton. Later, when the Spaniards were housed in their quarters, strange and exotic food was brought. Women were sent to cook and they prepared fish and fowls, dog meat with chili, and they cooked corn tortillas. Mangos and pineapples were served, as well as papayas from the great groves of Moctezuma, and many other fresh fruits. The Spaniards rested and waited for the arrival of Moctezuma.

When he arrived it was with great pomp. Six men carried him on a litter of gold and precious stones. The priests came first, then the governors of Moctezuma, the dwarfs of the court, and many other dignitaries. Drums were sounded, and the music of flutes filled the air. Beyond them a throng of people of the city waited anxiously, as they knew their priest-king had gone to meet the fabled Captain and his army, whom many believed to be gods. The air was charged; neither side knew what to expect. Certainly, the Aztecs did not want war with the gods who had come from across the eastern sea.

"Great ruler," the Captain greeted Moctezuma. "We come in peace, sent by our Majesty Don Carlos and his Governor to greet you."

"Malinche, I have heard of your deeds," Moctezuma answered, calling the Captain by the name of his interpreter. They knew she had many powers, and they believed she was a goddess.

The talk between the two leaders began, and as Malinche interpreted their words, she wondered what would happen to these two great men in the future.

In the days to come the soldiers would take Moctezuma prisoner. The Aztec warriors, uncertain and unguided, would hesitate to attack. Moctezuma would be killed, and his brother would lead an uprising against the Spaniards.

Fighting for their lives, the Spanish soldiers would be driven from the city, leaving many of their numbers dead on that fateful Noche Triste.

Eventually the army of the Captain, aided by the Indian enemies of the Aztecs, would reenter the city. Mexico-Tenochtitlan would fall, and the Aztec Empire would begin to crumble.

In the months ahead Malinche's sons would be born in Tenochtitlan. She would make sure they were brought up in the old traditions.

All this Malinche did not know as she stood between the two leaders and translated their words. But she was wise, and she knew that two men as powerful as the Captain and Moctezuma could not rule jointly. In this she was correct. The New World would not have two rulers, only one, and the Captain had planned his strategy well. His plan was to divide and conquer each Indian tribe he met, and he had the military advantage with his muskets, cannon and horsemen.

Because he had been expected as a god, the Captain won the battles of conquest. He did not rule as a god, however. He ruled as a man who would be Emperor of the New World.

THE CHILDREN

Time passed and Malinche grew accustomed to the city of Mexico. She came to know the Aztec people well. They, in turn, admired and respected her great powers. Her sons had been born in the Aztec city, and she gave them Aztec names. According to the prophecy of the shaman, she brought them up in the ways of the people of the city.

The Spaniards destroyed every temple and place of worship of the natives following their conquest of the Aztec capital city, but one temple remained hidden. It was built underground and a secret entrance was concealed within the living quarters of the priests. These quarters were located behind the main marketplace, and through them entered those who kept the old ways and went to pray to the gods of the Aztecs. It was there Malinche took her sons as soon as they were three, so they could receive instruction from the priests in the religion of the ancestors of Tenochtitlan. Malinche took them to the temple in secret because her husband had forbidden the practice of the ancient religion by any of her people.

Malinche's two sons brought her happiness even though she lived in a strange land. The Captain

spent much of his time in the provinces and in the
outlying villages consolidating his rule over the
country, so she spent most of her time with her
sons. In the mornings when she went to the marketplace she took them with her, wrapped in her rebozo.
The vendors of the marketplace grew to know the
two boys, and admired them greatly. The priests
told her that the boys had been born under a good
sign. They said that these two boys were born to
fulfill a great legacy. The people whispered and
nodded approvingly when they saw Olin and Tizoc
with their mother. They gave them gifts and honored
their mother.

In the afternoons Malinche sat in the shade of the
trees in the garden, relating stories to the boys.
She told them about the great Cacique who was their
grandfather, and about her journey to Mexico, and
how she had met the great Moctezuma. She taught
them the pantheon of Aztec gods as well as about
the Christ of the Spaniards. The boys listened
attentively as they learned the history of the
people of Mexico.

The boys grew tall and sturdy. One day, when the
Captain was home, he told Malinche that his sons
were destined to be great soldiers. He had two
swords made of wood so the boys could practice sword
play.

"Come now!" he shouted. "Learn to be soldiers.
When you are grown you will ride on horseback!" He
put the wooden swords in their hands and pushed
them at each other.

"I don't want to fight my brother," Tizoc said.
It was his nature to be gentle.

"You must practice, to make your bodies strong,"
the Captain insisted.

"We practice at the ball court," Olin said
proudly. He enjoyed exercise and the way of the
warrior.

"It's true," Malinche said, "every day they play
at the ball court. Look how strong they have become."

The ancient ball game of the Aztecs was a rigorous sport. It stretched the limbs and hardened the muscles.

"That's a silly game," the Captain said.

"All of our great warriors play in the ball courts," Malinche replied.

"And look what we did to them with our swords," the Captain laughed. "No, if you're to be a soldier of his Majesty, you need practice in sword play. Come now, like this!" He took the weapon from Tizoc and commanded Olin to charge him. He would show him how to parry and thrust. Olin did not hesitate. He feinted to the left then struck as hard as he could. The blow caught the Captain on the wrist. Letting out a cry, he dropped his sword, for he had not expected such a strong, sudden blow.

"Foul blow!" he cried and gripped his wrist.

"You forced him," Malinche said and drew her sons to her. "He didn't want to practice with your swords."

The Captain frowned. "They shall learn!" he said angrily. "What good are sons if they don't become soldiers? We have much work left to do in conquering these lands in the name of His Majesty. A man needs sons who are conquerors." With that he stalked away.

"I apologize," Olin said after him, but his father did not acknowledge him.

"It wasn't your fault," Malinche soothed her son.

"I think it was," Olin said and looked at her with clear, sincere eyes. "You have taught us not to fight, you have taught us the way of peace, and Tizoc seems to understand. The priests compliment him because already he can compose songs and read from the old writings. But I, I feel brave and strong when I am on the ball court, playing hard to win. Perhaps I should be a warrior, and not a man of peace like my brother." Having said this he walked away, still questioning the sudden urge that had driven him to strike so hard at his father's sword.

Malinche sighed. She watched her son walk away and remembered the prophecy of the old shaman: One son would be a wise and noble man of peace, the other would be a warrior.

THE LAKE

During those first seven years in Tenochtitlan many things occupied Malinche's time and energy. More Spaniards had arrived from Cuba, and they joined the ranks of those in Mexico. With them came more friars in long flowing gowns, men who destroyed all the native temples they could find and forced the Indians to accept the new religion. With them came the messengers who delivered letters from His Majesty in Spain. Don Carlos was pleased to receive the King's fifth of all the gold which was collected in the New World, but now it was time that the Captain returned to court to clear his name. The Governor of New Spain had accused the Captain of disloyalty. The Captain was ordered to appear at court to defend his actions.

Malinche knew the Captain had delayed his return to Spain by writing the King that his presence was needed in the new land to control the restless natives. Yes, he would return to court, but only after his hold on the New World was complete. He assured the king that everything he did was in the name of His Majesty, and when he returned to

Spain he would be able to offer riches beyond belief.

A famine had come upon the land, and one night a delegation of poor people came to Malinche.

"Malintzin, beloved of your people, we come to plead with you," the people said. "The soldiers have taken our corn and beans, and many of the fields are destroyed. Now there is hunger among the people. We beg you to help us."

"It is not right that you should suffer because of the war," Malinche answered. "You are farmers who tend your fields, and now the wars of conquest have touched your lives. Come with me."

She took the hungry people to the warehouses of the city, and she commanded that a portion of corn be given to them. The people were grateful and praised her name to the gods.

When the Captain heard this he was very angry. He wanted no one to counteract his orders. He knew the people loved Malinche and respected her. There was nothing they wouldn't do for her. He resented this favor she had with the people of the city.

During those same years many of the Indians died from smallpox, as they had no protection against the disease. For a long time the entire city was in mourning as they buried their dead. It was a very sad time. Malinche, because she knew many of the herbs and remedies for healing, went to the houses of the sick to aid them. A compassionate Spanish friar told her that if each person was inoculated, infected with a little of the disease, that person would later be immune to the illness. This was done and many lives were saved, but not before the disease had taken a devastating toll and weakened the population of the city and the provinces.

So the seven years at Tenochtitlan were filled not only with raising her two sons, but in helping the people recover from the ravages of conquest followed by disease. Malinche had discovered early that she loved the city of the Aztecs and its people. True, the Aztecs had been a warring nation and had exacted tributes from many towns, but among them were also the common and ordinary people who led a simple life and sustained the life of the city. A favorite place was the marketplace. Here the people of the city and from the provinces came together to sell their wares. But Malinche's favorite, quiet place was by the edge of the lake near one of the great causeways which led to the mainland.

Since her arrival, Malinche had been fascinated by the rich waters of the lake. In a way, they reminded her of the sea she had known as a child. But the dark brown waters of the lake were calm, and at sunset the lake glowed with a silver sheen. Here she could pass a quiet, reflective time. The water of the lake soothed her. Overhead the birds swirled and cried; she watched the swift swallows that never landed, scooping up water and mud to build their nests on the church walls. Here her sons could swim and play. The only people who passed were the fishermen in their canoes, and other traders who used the waterways to move their supplies from one city to the other. These people always waved to the woman and two children on the shore.

Malinche and her sons made another discovery. At that edge of the lake, near some rocks, and protected by a growth of bullrushes, there was a peaceful pond. There, in the clear water of the spring, they found a school of golden fish, fish so big and bright with orange scales that Malinche thought she had never seen anything as beautiful. This was a secret place she shared with her sons, and each day they went to the edge of the lake, taking with them some of the maize tortillas which they cut into small pieces and fed to the golden fish.

No fishermen approached this area of the lake. They knew about the golden fish that swam

there, and they knew the golden fish were not to
be disturbed. That area of the lake was a sacred
spot, for it was there the first Mexicans, the fore-
fathers of the Aztecs, had seen an eagle with a
snake in its beak, standing atop a giant nopal.
This was the sign which meant that on that small
island they should build their city, a city and an
empire which grew to rival all others.

A PRINCESS

Many of the soldiers who came with the Captain married Indian women, others married the Spanish women who began to come in the ships from across the sea. These women were fair, not dark like the Indian women, but some adopted the ways of the Indian and lived close to the Indian homes. They learned the customs of the Indians, they cooked the foods which were common to the inhabitants of Mexico, and some learned the language in order to trade in the marketplace. But most of the Spanish women wished to live in a separate part of the city, apart from the Indian population. They rode in big carriages when they went to the market, and they used their servants to do all their bartering and buying.

Malinche knew these women did not approve of her. She heard them whisper behind her back. They laughed at her and criticized the Captain. Malinche couldn't understand their behavior, but she went on doing her work as before. The women envied her because she was married to the Captain who had become a powerful ruler, the Governor and Adelantado of Mexico; and some feared her because she had so much

power with the Indians.   It was secretly whispered
that without her the Captain could never rule the
city, much less the provinces where there was always
unrest.

Then one day on a great ship there came a woman
whom everybody called the Princess Isabela.   She was
a very important person in the court of the King.
She had come as a special envoy of the King to per-
suade the Captain to return to Spain, and the Captain
himself had made the trip from Mexico to the coastal
town to receive her and escort her back to Mexico.

She was a beautiful young woman, charming and
quick to smile.   She always dressed in a flowing
gown, while carrying a silk fan in her hand.   She
was fair and lively, witty in her conversation, and
a flirt with the officers.   They all bowed when
she walked by, and each soldier considered it a
special honor to escort her to mass on Sundays or
on her visits around the city.

One afternoon, shortly after the arrival of the
Princess, the twins found their mother in the garden
of their home.   It was near the time for the Feast
of Flowers, and Malinche was dressed in a long,
white gown made of cotton.   Her huipil was also
white, but embroidered with the green feathers of
the quetzal bird, such feathers as were reserved
only for royalty.   On her head she wore a gold
crown, a gift from Moctezuma.

"Mother," Olin called when they saw her.   "It
is time to go to the lake to feed the fish."

Malinche turned and smiled at her sons.   They
were only seven, but already they were ready to
go to the ceremony at the temple which would
make them men in the eyes of the people.   They
were handsome boys, of noble bearing, destined,
Malinche was sure, to be great leaders.

"I cannot go with you now," Malinche answered.
"Today the chiefs and caciques from the provinces
are to meet with the Captain.   I must be at his
side to interpret for him.   You know well it is

the time of the Feast of Flowers. Today, if all
goes well, there may finally be peace throughout
the land. It is important that I be present, I
have promised your father."

"But we thought he was away with the soldiers,"
Tizoc said.

"He returned last night," Malinche answered.

"He is seldom with us," Olin said.

"He has great responsibilities," Malinche told
her sons. "The people are unhappy and dissent
continues in the provinces; as he is the Governor
he must go with the soldiers. But now maybe a
lasting peace will come to the land."

"How can it be peace if it is based on harsh
rules?" Tizoc asked.

Malinche put her arms around her sons and
together they sat on a garden bench. "Life has
been hard since the Spaniards came," she said.
"But before they arrived the tribes were splintered
into warring groups. Maybe now we can hope there
will be unity, and so out of our suffering may
come some good. We must have peace and unity,
because that is the only way we will survive.
The Spaniard with his cannons, muskets, swords
and horse cavalry is too powerful to resist. The
resistance now, and in the future, is in you,
my sons."

"But the priest says that the day of the old
warriors is gone," Olin added. "How can I be a
warrior for my people if the old ways are dead?"

"Time changes everything," Malinche answered.
"It is for us to find a way to live in the new
era. We have been forced to give up our religion
and many of our customs, we have been made
slaves in our own land, and many have died of
the new diseases brought by the Spaniard. But
we have survived, and it is up to us to retain
what we see as truth in our lives. It will
not be easy."

"Is that why you are sad, mother?" asked Tizoc.

"Yes," Malinche replied.   "When I first saw these men from across the sea I thought they brought a new and better life to our people, that the new age of Quetzalcoatl was here.   I did not believe they were gods, but I did believe that they had the capacity to create a new age.   That is why I aided your father, and I was by his side throughout our march to Mexico.   I kept believing that a golden age would dawn.   Even when war was waged, I thought that a new harmony would come from it. But I was wrong.   The time will never be the same as when I was a child."

"But what if the wise and noble god, Quetzalcoatl, were to return?" Tizoc asked.   The boy excelled in songs and poetry, and the priests said he was bound to be a wise ruler.

Malinche turned away.   In the distance she could see the snow-clad tops of the sleeping volcanos which lay to the southeast.   She felt a cold breeze on her skin.   What if the god were to return?   Would he recognize his people, the once proud Aztecs, now conquered?   But hope was something which could not be stamped out, even with the changes that time brought.

"Perhaps that is the only hope left for Mexico," she said, "that the wise god return, he who creates harmony between heaven and earth. Or it may be he will come in the form of a man, or a woman, some poor person who rises from the earth of our land and comes to show the people the way.   That hope will always be there. I see it in the eyes of the people as they come to the church to worship."

She paused.   They heard the sounds of drums and flutes.   The Captain and the entourage of chiefs were arriving.   Now the talks would begin.

"Go," she said to her sons, "go to the lake without me.   Your father is coming.   Now it's time for the affairs of state.   I will come shortly."

The boys kissed their mother, then ran out of

the garden towards the lake. Malinche turned to
face the procession which came through the wide
gate of the garden. First came the Spanish drummers,
then the guards and soldiers dressed in bright
colored pantaloons with breastplates of armor
covering their chests, their pointed helmets shining
in the sun. They strutted as they walked, their
bright swords hanging by their sides, the long
muskets over their shoulders.

Behind them came the Indian guards, some
playing the shrill clay flutes and shaking dry
gourd rattles, the rest carrying shields with the
sign of their war god painted on thick leather.
Each warrior was armed with bow and arrows and
war clubs which were studded with black obsidian
points on either side. They walked proudly, too,
because their duty was to protect the chiefs of
the people, and because some of them had not
yet surrendered to the Spaniards.

The scene was resplendent with color and sound.
The high notes of the flutes sounded above the
slow, measured roll of the drums. The guards
marched smartly, as if trying to outdo each other.
Behind them came the friars of the church and
the priests of the people. The advisors of the
chiefs followed behind each cacique. Each chief
was clothed in garments made of cotton embroidered
with feathers. All was bright and royal.

The women of the city, already preparing for
the Feast of Flowers, came in front, spreading
flowers of every color before the marchers.
The perfume of the flowers filled the air. Some
of the Spanish women had joined the march, dressed
in their brocaded gowns with their hair done up
in loops and curls. They carried silk fans to
cool themselves in the stifling heat. There
was an air of pomp in the procession, but also
an air of gaiety. A real fiesta was beginning,
and with it came the promise of a lasting peace.

Finally the Captain appeared. He was dressed

in elegant splendor.   He wore a cloak of brocade
and silk with pantaloons of velvet.   His sword was
encased in a scabbard of gold, a present from one
of the villages.   Both the scabbard and his helmet
shone in the sun.   His reddish beard was neatly
trimmed, and his bright eyes were aware of the
smallest detail.   He walked proudly, a soldier and
a conqueror who now wanted peace.

When Malinche caught sight of him, her heart
was filled with pride and love.   He was a handsome
man.   Even with her doubts and concerns over the
wars he had waged with her people, she still
loved him.   She felt her heart beat faster when
she saw him, and as he felt her gaze, he looked
toward her and smiled.   Then the Princess Isabela
appeared.   The Captain held out his arm for her
and together they came forward.

When Malinche saw the Princess she felt jealousy.
It was she who should be walking at the side of
her husband, not the foreign Princess from across
the sea.   The Princess was beautiful with her
pale skin and elegant attire.   It was evident
the Captain admired her.   Malinche knew the Princess had been sent to try to lure the Captain
back to Spain.

The Captain had made enemies when he disobeyed
the Governor of Cuba, and the letters of condemna-
tion about the Captain's actions had reached
the King himself.   There were many jealous dukes
and princes in the court who thought the Captain
had gone too far in his conquest and who thought
he was too powerful.   This is what they whispered
to the King, that the Captain was setting himself up as a king of the New World, and that
he was dangerous.   He should be punished.   Malinche knew it was not safe for the Captain
to return to Spain, but now the Princess had
come with all sorts of inducements to lure him
back.

The procession stopped as it neared Malinche.

The Captain held up his arm for the drums and flutes to cease.

"My dear Malinche," the Captain said. "The chiefs of all the great nations of Mexico have come to sue for peace. But before the talks begin, it is only right we entertain them. We are on our way to the ballcourt to see the games. Will you join us?"

Malinche felt distracted. How could they have time for games when things in the provinces were going so badly.

"My Prince," she answered. "I am not in the mood for games. Every day more and more people flock into the city from the provinces. They flee the wars, and they are hungry."

"You worry too much," the Captain replied. "We all want peace, that is why this meeting with the chiefs was called."

"I think peace will only come when the Indian tribes are under complete control and pay allegiance to the Governor, our Captain," the Princess said and smiled at the Captain.

"That is the peace we must have," the Captain nodded. He turned to Malinche. "May I present the Princess Isabela from Castile, an envoy of His Majesty the King."

The Princess nodded, Malinche acknowledged her.

"I understand you are returning to Spain," Malinche said.

"Yes, there is a ship waiting for me at port. In a few days I shall take my leave. And I must say I shall be glad to leave this savage land. It has only one saving grace."

"And what is that?" asked Malinche.

The Princess looked coyly at the Captain. "I have had the honor to meet the conqueror of New Spain, the great Captain General and Governor of Mexico. All of the civilized world is talking about his exploits. His Majesty the King wants him to return so he may bestow favors on this brave and gallant knight."

"But he has no intention of returning to Spain," Malinche said as she looked at the Captain. He turned his face away.

"Oh, he must go," the Princess crooned. "The King has great plans for him, he will receive many honors. It isn't every day a man has a kingdom ready to bow at his feet. This is his opportunity, and he must take advantage of it."

"Well," the Captain coughed, "perhaps we can discuss this at some other time."

"There isn't much time left," the Princess said. Her voice grew irritated. "In court you can have anything you desire, here you have only a barbaric country full of conquered savages. They don't appreciate nor understand what you have tried to do for them. You brought them civilization and the Christian faith, and in return they make war against you."

"The people of this land had their own civilization long before the Spaniard came," Malinche answered sharply. "They make war to preserve their freedom. And as for savages..."

"Oh, how rude of me," the Princess interrupted her. "I had forgotten that you are..."

"A savage?"

"No, a native," the Princess said haughtily. "You were born here, so you understand the ways of the heathen. I could never live here. I much prefer the civilized ways of the court. And I'm sure the Captain would prefer it too. Now I must take my leave, I have much to do to prepare for my journey."

"But the ball game?" the Captain muttered.

"It's really too hot to sit through that boring game," the Princess told him. "Please excuse me."

She held out her hand as the Captain bowed and kissed it. He walked with her to the gate of the garden.

"Will I see you?" the Princess asked.

"Yes, just as we agreed," the Captain smiled. The Princess turned and walked away, her maids scurrying after her.

The Captain turned to Malinche. "A very adventurous young Princess," he said.

"Yes," Malinche answered, "very adventurous. It seems she is determined to have you return to Spain."

"It had been on my mind, but I hadn't seriously considered it, until..."

"Until the Princess came?"

"Yes," the Captain nodded. He grew excited as he spoke. "You must realize what it means if His Majesty receives me. The old accusations of the Governor of Cuba will be cleared. I will be made a Lord, my deeds recognized..."

"Your deeds are recognized here," Malinche reminded him. "Is that not enough? Why do you need a title from the court when you are already Governor of this country. You have many enemies in the Spanish court, men who want to see you in prison."

"The King's pardon would dispel all those rumors," the Captain answered. "The Princess has told me that those who plot against me have no power. Don't you see, the King plans to reward me for my conquests. That has always been my dream. To be recognized for my deeds as a conquistador!"

"Was that your only dream?"

"Yes," he answered. He grew excited as he thought of the prospects of returning to Spain. He had forgotten the chiefs who waited patiently in the garden to continue to the ballcourt. As he spoke, what was most important to him was his dream of glory in the royal court.

"The King is ready to recognize me," he said to himself.

"And what of your family?" Malinche asked.

"I will take my sons with me, of course," was the answer.

"No, you cannot take my sons!" Malinche gasped.
His quick and ready answer caught her by surprise.
She had realized that perhaps sometime the Captain
would decide to return to Spain, and she was ready
to accept that, but she had not thought, not even
in her most secret fears, that he would take her
sons with him. That could not be, it was unthink-
able. Without her sons she would die.

"Of course I can," the Captain said forcefully.
"They are my sons. If I decide to return to Spain
they shall go with me. It is right for them to see
their father's homeland. They bear my name, they
will inherit my rewards."

Malinche grasped his arm. "You can't mean
what you've said. I don't believe my ears. You
wouldn't take my children from me!"

He pulled his arm free, then whispered. "You're
making a scene, and we have guests." He looked
towards the chiefs who had turned to look at the
two when they heard Malinche's voice rise. She
nodded and stepped back, aware that in front of
the great Mexican chiefs she must keep her dignity.

"That's better," the Captain smiled. "No sense
to upset our guests. Things are very touchy as
they are. I knew you would understand. I tell
you, my mind is made up on this issue. My
sons must return to receive a proper Christian
education. I know you have taken them in secret
to the heathen priests, but now all that will
change. They will leave this land of savages—."

He stopped quickly when he realized what he
had said. Malinche looked at him bitterly. "Then
I, too, am a savage...."

"I didn't mean that," the Captain quickly
said. "I have always known you are an intelli-
gent woman. But you must think what is best
for our sons. Here your own people don't accept
them, because they are not pure Indians. In
Spain they will be noblemen."

"They are noble men to me," Malinche answered.

"They don't need titles for that. Your need for titles, gold and conquest will destroy your own honor, but you don't see that."

She stepped back and looked at the Captain. He was the most powerful man in Mexico, and she had helped him achieve that power. Without her he could not have accomplished his goal, but he had used her love and her gifts wrongly. Now she would have to be strong to fight for her sons.

"If my honor is to suffer, then so will yours," the Captain said. "You were my ally. You were at my side throughout the early days, during the march to Tlaxcala and Cholula, and here to Mexico where we met the great Moctezuma. You interpreted for me, so my words were yours. Don't you see, among your people there are already some who whisper your name, and to them Malinche means traitor!"

Malinche winced at his words. She wanted to fight, to strike back, but she knew what he said was true. If a history were ever written of these times, there would be many who would brand her as a traitor for what she had done.

"But come now, forget all that," the Captain said. "Come to the ballcourt, enjoy the games. The Feast of Flowers begins, and later we will need to speak to the assembled chiefs."

Malinche felt weak and helpless as she looked at the Captain. How, after his unkind words, could he still ask her help? It was her skill which had aided the Captain and his soldiers to conquer Mexico. She was partly to blame for the wars, the years of famine, the smallpox which had almost devastated the Indians. And all this she had done because of her love for this man.

"Are you all right?" the Captain asked. He noticed her pallor and saw her trembling.

She nodded, gathering a reserve of strength from within. "Go without me," she said.

The Captain shrugged. "Very well," he said. He turned and gave the signal to begin the drums and flutes again, then motioned to the waiting chiefs. The procession then moved through the garden to make its way to the ballcourt.

Malinche remained alone in the garden. Her mind was filled with the happenings of the past. She remembered the first time she had met the Captain, and how much she admired and loved him. She had truly believed that if her people joined forces with him and his men, he would bring peace to the land. But she had been misled, and now she felt a terrible shame. Now he planned to take her sons from her. Perhaps that was her punishment, but no, she could not allow such a thing to happen. Her sons would be made slaves, mistreated and looked upon as savages from a strange land. That is what would happen, and she could not help but see the Princess as the one behind all this plotting. The woman did not like Indians. It was she who had put these ideas in the Captain's mind, and if Malinche allowed it, her sons would be taken away from her.

Malinche straightened her shoulders. She had never been a weak woman, and she would not be weak now. Weakness was what had caused the fall and death of Moctezuma, and as father to his people he had failed. Malinche would not fail. Better death than to see her sons live in shame. Quickly she left the garden, but she didn't go to join the celebrants at the ballcourt. She could hear their shouts as the game began. She stole across the back streets of the city towards the old temple and knocked stealthily at the north entrance. An old priest opened the door and allowed her to enter.

THE WAR GOD

"Enter, my child," the old priest said. Other
priests were waiting in the dark. One handed her
a candle, then they turned and led the way through
a dark, damp tunnel. They moved towards the
center of the temple, the central room where the
giant statues of the gods waited. Malinche knew
only the most trusted were allowed into this last
and secret temple of the city. The Spaniards
had destroyed the rest, while this one had been
saved because it had been built underground, and
even now it was threatened because of the seepage
of water from the surrounding lake. There was
no way to carry on repairs without the Spaniards
knowing.

When they entered the large chamber the priests
lighted the fires in braziers. An eerie light
filled the huge room. Beautiful mosaics and
paintings which recorded the history and ceremonies of the Aztecs covered the walls. Many
of the old gods were painted in all their splendor.
But the center of attraction were the two huge
statues which dominated the room. One was the

statue of the War God, Huitzilopochtli, the other
was the god of culture and light, Quetzalcoatl.
Always before Malinche had prayed first at the
statue of Quetzalcoatl, now the priests were surprised to see her approach the War God.

It was a huge statue, carved from hard volcanic
rock, the harsh visage looking down on the suppli-
cant, the trembling and lonely Malinche. Adorned
with precious stones and gold, the War God held
a club in one hand, a shield in the other. His
countenance seemed to say, what do you want of me?
Pitiful woman, traitor of your people, peace-lover
who has forgotten to pray to me and instead
offers incense and words of love to my brother.
What do you want of me? Why do you come to me
now?

The priests sensed the urgency of Malinche's
step. They quickly put the resin on the embers
of the brazier, the copal burned brightly and
filled the large chamber with sweet smoke. Then
they bowed and retired, leaving Malinche alone
to pray to the god. Malinche looked into the
face of the War God, saw his frown, understood
why he should rebuke her and not answer her
prayers. Nevertheless, she prayed, beseeching
the god for help in her most dire hour of need.

"God of War, god of the Aztecs, make me strong,
I pray," she said aloud. "I pray to you, guide
me on the right path, guide my steps. I have
neglected you, now I pray for forgiveness.
All I have done I renounce, I place myself in
your hands. Reveal to me if now is the time to
destroy the conqueror of our people. The day
must come, we cannot live in slavery forever.
Tell me if now is the time! Tell me what I must
do to atone for my wrongs and gain the freedom
of my people!"

On and on Malinche prayed, repeating her im-
precations, revealing to the god her role in the
conquest of the Aztec Empire by the Spaniards.

"I believed he would bring peace. I loved him. I bore him sons, and now he threatens to take them away from me."

She stopped. She couldn't go on, it was almost impossible for her to see and admit her responsibility in the subjugation of her people by the Spaniards. Then she found her strength and raised her arms in supplication.

"I helped him conquer this world. I taught him the way, I was at his side when he met the Indian nations of our world. I became a traitor to my own people. That is what I am called by some, la Malinche, the traitor. It is I who condemned my people to slavery, I betrayed you. I did it because I believed in peace, I truly believed the time had come for this great leader to bring a lasting peace. I loved this man, this leader Moctezuma called a god even unto his death. I fell in love with him and betrayed my people and my gods!"

Her cry of anguish echoed in the chamber. Her heart ached when she thought of the man she loved. Then she made herself strong and cried out again.

"Now make my heart strong! Enter my heart and guide me in your ways!"

The embers in the brazier sputtered and rose, casting a dancing light and shadows in the dim chamber. A faint tremor seemed to pass through the earth, the giant statue of the War God seemed to move.

"Give me a sign! Tell me what I must do!" Malinche cried.

She looked up and through the smoke of the incense she saw a knife in the hand of the god. She trembled, then drew near. It was the sign she had asked for, and she understood its meaning. First she shook her head and exclaimed, "No!" It could not be that this was the god's answer. In her mind she heard the voice of the god.

You have asked for a sign, and it has been given!
You must obey the will of the God of War.

Malinche nodded.   She reached forward and took
the black obsidian knife from the hand of the god.
This was the god's sign, the sharp knife which
shone brightly in the light of the fire.   She
pressed it to her breast, then she bowed and walked
fearfully from the temple.

ATTEMPT TO ESCAPE

That night Malinche slept fitfully; nightmares filled her mind. In a vision she saw her sons at the marketplace. They drew close to the other Indian boys who were engaged in a ball game, but they were not invited to play. Instead, the Indian boys taunted them and cried, "Half-bloods! Half-bloods don't play the game of warriors!" And so, among her own people, her sons would always be known as mestizos, the half-breed sons of a Spanish man and an Indian woman. The dream tore at Malinche's heart.

In another vision she saw her sons in chains, slaves in the dark hold of a ship which tossed dangerously on high seas. Somewhere the face of the Princess appeared, laughing shrilly. Other dreams pressed on her thoughts, scenes of long lines of Indians, all in chains, all suffering for want of food. She saw again the burial processions which had filled the city during the epidemic of smallpox. Darkness and stench filled the air, and hovering over every scene which flashed in her mind she saw the sharp, obsidian dagger she had received from the War God.

To save her sons, to save her sanity, she had to act. In the first light of dawn she arose and dressed quickly. She had decided to flee the city, to escape the tyrant Captain, to put the past behind her, return to her people on the coast and start a new life. It was the only way to escape the cruel prophecy of the god.

"What is it?" Olin asked as she entered their room, awakening them with her fingers on their lips so they would not scream.

"Dress quickly," she told them. "We're going on a journey."

The boys obeyed, dressed quickly and followed their mother into the garden. They didn't know where they were going or why they had been roused out of bed at such an early hour, but the urgency in their mother's voice told them to trust and to obey.

The sun was just rising in the east, gilding the valley in a harsh, cold light. As they stepped into the street they saw the workers who already filled the streets. Carpenters and masons walked toward the construction sites where the Spaniards were building new homes. Some would go to the site of the new cathedral. A woman vendor with a basket of flowers balanced on her head appeared, followed by another with a load of hot corn tortillas. The woman would stop at every door and the cook or maid would come out to buy the hot tortillas for the breakfast meal. Other vendors from the provinces moved towards the marketplace, their baskets laden with produce. But an advancing storm pressed down on them as Malinche and her sons made their way towards the lake.

As the city was surrounded by water, the only exit was across the causeways. Malinche knew that Spanish guards were posted at the entrance of each causeway, but she was not prepared for the confrontation which followed.

"Be brave," she whispered to her sons as they approached the guards on station. There was only one thing to do, to challenge the guards and hope they suspected nothing.

"Buenos días, Doña Marina," the sergeant of the guards said as she and her sons drew near.

"Buenos días, señor," Malinche answered. She knew the soldier, an honest and respected man. Behind him stood two more soldiers who cautiously checked the baskets of each of the vendors who was coming into the city from the provinces. The causeway was crowded with vendors, and at the gate a group stood around the entrance station, eager to receive the advance signal from the soldiers so they could hurry to the marketplace. The vendors at the check point recognized Malinche and turned to look at her and her sons. What brought the noble Malinche to the causeway so early in the morning?

"A busy morning," Malinche said, meaning the crowd of vendors.

"Everyone wants a good place in the market for the Feast of Flowers, señora," the sergeant smiled. "Some say even at this early hour there is no place left in the great market, so they plan to camp here and sell."

Many of the vendors had set their wares on the ground near the entrance. Here, they would do their trading. This was the marketplace of the poor and the lame, those who were not quick enough to get to the central marketplace. They would receive no gold coins from selling to the Spanish maids, but they would do their own trading among their own people. All turned when Malinche approached.

"Do you come to trade here?" the sergeant asked.

"No," Malinche responded calmly. "My sons and I go to visit relatives in the provinces."

She stepped forward, but the sergeant did not

step out of her path.   "It is a long walk, Doña
Marina," the guard said.

"Yes.   So we have started early.   If you will
be so kind as to let us pass."

Her voice was stern, but the guard did not move.
"I am afraid I cannot do that, señora," he said.

"You cannot let us pass?" Malinche asked.   Her
voice rose in anger..

"I have my orders, señora.   You are not to leave
the city."

"Who gave those orders?" Malinche asked.   Her
voice rose but inside she trembled.   She knew she was
trapped.

"The orders came directly from the Captain General.
Every gate has been ordered not to allow you or
your sons to pass."

"I am a free woman," Malinche said aloud.   "I
may come and go as I wish."

She stepped forward again, but the sergeant
raised his hand and instantly the other guards jumped
forward, their hands on their swords.   Malinche's
sons stepped to her side, surprised by the actions
of the guards.   The vendors around the gate also
rose, sensing the confrontation taking place; they
drew their machetes from their belts, ready to
protect this woman they knew and admired.   A tense
silence filled the air.

Malinche looked into the guard's eyes and
sensed his fear.   One word from her and the vendors
would attack, the path of escape would be clear.
But that would mean a battle, injury and death,
the very thing she blamed on the Spanish soldiers.
She shook her head, turned to the vendors and
spoke in their native language, telling them she
had changed her mind, she would respect the order
not to leave.   The men nodded and retired to their
business, but still keeping an eye on the soldiers.

"Very well," Malinche said to the guard.   "So be
it.   I will not leave the city."

The sergeant breathed a sigh of relief.   He had

not relished a fight with the vendors, even though they were armed only with machetes.

"Thank you, Doña Marina.   I hope you understand that it isn't for lack of respect that we do this. We don't know what is going on, or why the orders came.   But we have the orders from the Captain General himself, and we must obey them."

Malinche nodded, turned and took her sons by the hand and walked away. She walked as proud and noble as a queen, but she felt her knees weaken. Her plan was thwarted, she had been naive to think she could escape. She realized she was being backed into a corner from which there was no escape.

"Why are we forbidden to leave the city?" Tizoc asked.

"It is a game the Captain plays," she said calmly so as not to alarm them.

The game was becoming deadly serious; in her anger she had underestimated the Captain, and her mistake might prove to be disastrous. She should have known that he would block her escape route. He was determined to take her children from her, and he would use all the power at his disposal. Now she was trapped with no one to whom she could turn. She was cut off from her family, a prisoner in her own home. The anger flared like fire in her breast. What could she do?

She remembered the temple visit, and the dagger the God of War had given her. Was that her only alternative? The thought caused her to shudder with fear.

BETRAYAL

In her desperation to find a solution, Malinche thought, perhaps there was one person who might help, one who could make the Captain change his mind. The Princess Isabela. Surely the Princess would be compassionate, she would understand the natural love and concern a mother has for her children. Malinche vowed to swallow her pride and go to the Princess. It was her last hope, and for her sons she would do anything.

This was what Malinche was thinking as she and her sons drew near the living quarters of the Princess. A day and night had passed since her visit to the temple, and Malinche had not slept. She felt tired and angry. The once proud Malinche no longer walked stately like a queen. Her hair was in disarray and her feet were muddy from the walk to the lake. She seemed not to notice, for now, as she hurried, pulling her sons behind her, her thoughts were on the image of the War God offering her the sharp knife of sacrifice.

"Wait here," she told her sons as they approached the gate of the garden. The boys nodded and sat

down to wait.   They didn't understand the strange
change which had come over their mother, but they
sensed her anguish.   As boys who knew well the
tradition of warriors, they knew not to ask questions,
but to wait as they were ordered.

Malinche entered the garden of the quarters
of the Princess.   The sun was covered by clouds,
and the wind blew furiously.   Lightning flashed
in the darkened sky.   Malinche had gone only a
few steps when she heard the voices of the Captain
and the Princess.   She made her way cautiously
forward, keeping to the deep shade of the trees
and bushes so she would not be seen.   She spied the
Captain and the Princess seated near the fountain.

"I have heard the people say she is going mad,"
the Princess Isabela said.   She held her cape to
her face.

"Yes, she doesn't sleep, instead she roams
her sleeping quarters at night, seemingly tor-
mented by bad dreams.   I believe it has to do
with her religion from which I have tried to
dissuade her, but with no success."

"Where, then, are her supernatural powers?"
the Princess laughed.   "She sounds like a mere
woman to me, slave to her emotions, to her love
for you.   That's all it is, can't you see that?
She doesn't want to lose you.   She will keep
you tied to this primitive land forever if you
refuse to admit her influence."

"That's not what I fear," the Captain said.

Malinche realized they were talking about her.
She drew closer to listen.

"Fear?" the Princess asked.   "Did I hear the
great conqueror of the New World say he feared
this Indian woman?"

"That's not what I meant," the Captain replied.
"She does have a strong influence over people.
True, some consider her a traitor, but most know
her as a woman with great power.   She has aided
the natives for many years, and so she commands

their love and respect. They would do anything for her, including joining an insurrection."

"And you are afraid of war?" the Princess asked. "The Captain General of the New World afraid of war?"

The Captain nodded. "I am afraid of an uprising here in the city. We generally have control in the provinces, even though there is some resistance. Those small wars we can fight and win, and we can extend our control, but if an uprising occurred here in the city it would set us back many years. Most of my soldiers are in the provinces, my military strength is weak here. A war here would mean cancellation of the trip to Spain."

"I see," the Princess said, surprised by these implications. The Captain was right. To strengthen the grip of control one had to move with caution.

"Do you think she would lead the natives into war?"

"No, I don't think so. She has seen how war has devastated her people and the land. I don't think she would take the responsibility of war on her shoulders. Not now."

"I would," the Princess said coyly and placed her hand on the Captain's arm. "I would wage war for you."

"You have not seen war, my dear Princess," the Captain answered softly and took her hand in his.

"She hesitates to cross you because she still loves you," the Princess said. "But she is a mad woman. I suggest the best alternative is to have her thrown in prison, declare her insane and lock her away. You once imprisoned the great Moctezuma, and when the people saw he had lost his power as a ruler they turned against him. They will turn against Malinche also. That will take care of her threat."

"She can be imprisoned," the Captain said, "but her strange powers cannot. I have seen her perform acts that can only be explained as magic or of the supernatural. No, I have thought of another solution.   You know my friend, Captain Alvarado?"

"Yes, a handsome, brave soldier.   I understand he has been with you throughout the conquest, and one of your most trusted captains."

"He is.   And he has always admired and respected Malinche."

"Why are you telling me this?" the Princess asked.

"Because he is part of my solution," the Captain smiled.   "It is the custom of the natives to give their daughters to warriors they respect.   This often happens when treaties are made, to help cement the peace.   As you know, my marriage to Malinche was never blessed by vows in the church. You might say, she was like a gift to me.   I kept her, and treated her well," the Captain added.

"Go on."   The Princess was intrigued.

"I have been thinking, if she was a gift to me, I can also give her away as a gift.   So last night I went to my friend Alvarado and discussed this proposition with him.   I would give him Malinche, to keep in anyway he saw fit, but I would have control of my sons.   He agreed, of course, in fact he was very pleased by the prospect."

"What an excellent idea!" the Princess cried. "Now you are free to do as you will."

"Exactly," the Captain smiled again.   "And as I am following the custom of the natives, Malinche cannot oppose it.   She must live by the law of her people."

"Wonderful!" exclaimed the Princess as she drew close to the Captain.   As she did so she saw Malinche step out of the shadows of the trees. She gasped as Malinche approached them.

"What are you doing here?" the Captain cried harshly.

"Listening to your schemes," was her reply.   She drew near, the two stepped back as she approached. The sudden appearance of the disheveled woman surprised and shocked them.   Malinche's hair was

uncombed and her dress splattered with mud. There
was rage and cunning in her eyes. The Princess drew
her cape about her shoulders and turned as if to leave.

"Stop!" Malinche cried. "So, my noble husband,"
she said, eyeing the Captain, "you have devised a
plot to give me away, as a gift, as if I were nothing
more than your piece of property!" Her voice was
shrill and full of anger.

"Our marriage was never recognized by the church!"
the Captain countered.

"I have no need for your church rules or recogni-
tion!" Malinche shouted.

"I must protect my sons!" he answered.

"You have never shown concern for them! And now
if you separate me from them you will anger the
gods!" She spoke vehemently, but the Captain,
asserting himself, stepped forward.

"I don't fear your heathen gods!" he countered.
"They have no power over good Christians."

"I will go to my people," Malinche threatened.

"They recognize the custom," the Captain answered
quickly. "A man may put aside his wife. You will
be taken care of by Alvarado, there is nothing to
protest."

Malinche felt great anguish, as if the obsidian
knife she secretly carried was slicing through
her heart. The Captain was cunning, he had thought
through every step, so she must be calm, not let
them frighten her. She fell to her knees and took
the Captain's hands in hers.

"I beg you, noble Lord, do not take them from
me, or I will surely die." Then she turned to
the Princess. "Someday you will be a mother and
know the love a mother has for her children. I
beg you to understand my plight. To take my children
from me is like taking my heart. I cannot live
without my heart."

Her sweet words surprised them both. Before
the Captain could answer, the two boys who had
crept into the garden and hidden in the shrubs
came forward.

"My sons!" Malinche cried and rushed to them.

"What are they doing here?" the Captain shouted.

"We came with our mother," Olin answered.

"My, isn't it a regular family reunion," Princess Isabela said haughtily. "My dear Captain General, I have no time for these arguments. I must prepare to sail, and I will sail with or without you, my Lord. The wish of His Majesty is also clear, you are to return with your sons, and remember this, the offer of your pardon at the court may never again be repeated." She turned and quickly walked away.

"Wait!" the Captain called, but she was gone. He turned to Malinche. "See what you have done? Are you mad? Why parade my sons everywhere you go?"

"Ask them if they will go with you, or stay with me," Malinche said. "Let that be the test, not the wishes of a King we have never seen."

The Captain looked at his sons. They were growing tall and strong. It was true, he had not had time to be with them, the wars in the provinces had kept him busy. But they were his sons, and he wanted all that was best for them. Surely the King had a good reason for wanting to see them, surely he would grant them titles, perhaps land.

"Of course they will come with me," he said softly. "They are boys, but the journey will make men out of them. They will see a world other boys only dream of, the court of Spain, His Majesty the King. Here they have nothing. The Indians don't accept them because they have a Spaniard for a father, and the Spaniards..." He paused and thought a moment, and spoke to the boys. "They won't accept you either," he said. "We can only hope you will receive a title from the King. No one can take that from you. Do you understand?"

The two boys nodded.

"There! You see!" the Captain smiled. "They have agreed with me. They will go."

"We understand what you say," Olin interrupted,

"but we cannot go with you. Our life is here, our people are here. I have vowed to follow the path of the War God, because our people will always need warriors. Tizoc will follow the path of Quetzalcoatl, and the day the true god returns to our land to save it from conquest and ruin, then Tizoc will be here and know how to speak to this God of Light. That is why we must remain."

The Captain was stunned by the answer. He had never heard either of his sons speak so clearly and eloquently. Then his surprise turned to anger and he turned on Malinche.

"You have taught them this!" he shouted. "You have allowed the heathen priests to fill their minds with this nonsense! The boys will go with me, want to or not."

With this outburst he reached out and grabbed his sons by their arms. The boys resisted but were unable to free themselves.

"Have pity!" Malinche cried.

"Guards! Guards!" the Captain yelled, and two guards came running. "Take the woman away!" he commanded, and the guards took hold of Malinche.

"I beg you, one last favor!" she cried and ceased struggling. The two boys also grew still. "Listen to my last request," she said in a calm voice. "Allow me to say goodbye to my sons, to be with them a few hours."

The Captain looked at her suspiciously. He looked at the two guards who still held Malinche's arms. For a moment he felt ashamed that it took three grown men to subdue the woman and the boys.

"Guards," he commanded, "stand by the gate." The guards withdrew and the Captain turned to Malinche. "Very well, you may say your goodbye. But if I have to call the guards again, I will."

"My Lord," Malinche said, "I know you will not change your decision. I must abide by it."

The Captain smiled. "Now you're doing the right thing," he nodded.

"I have only one last request to make," Malinche said. "Allow me the time to talk to my sons, allow me to explain what needs to be done. They will understand, and comply. My poor creatures, they are frightened now, like fish caught in the net of the fisherman, they need to feel the freedom of the water. They don't understand this fierce struggle between the two of us, they only feel the terror. Perhaps if I could be with them a few hours, walk by the lake with them...."

The Captain shook his head.

"I beg you," Malinche continued, "before you say no, consider this last request I make. I give you my word, I will not attempt to escape. As you know, the gates of the city are guarded, and I have no wings to fly away. You did love me once...and I loved you. Surely you haven't forgotten."

The Captain hesitated. Her words were sweet, and she did vow not to flee. "Very well, I will grant you a few minutes, but on one condition: you will not attempt to escape."

Malinche looked at her sons. She touched their hair, and the deep love she had for them suddenly brought the image of the War God into her thoughts. She shivered with fear and her eyes filled with tears, but again she found her inner strength and answered calmly.

"I will not escape," she said sadly. "And as much as I love my sons, I will part with them."

"Swear by your gods," the Captain tested her.

Malinche choked, but her voice was clear. "I swear by the gods of my ancestors, I will part with my sons."

The Captain was pleased. She had finally come to her senses. The whole thing had become more complex than he wished. He had no desire to put the screaming boys aboard the ship, he didn't want the mad and raving Malinche crying and shouting in the streets of the city. That would only increase the possibility of an uprising. He did not want to risk fighting in the city as he was about to return to Spain to report to the King.

Yes, he thought, it is better to be patient and use a little prudence. Let her have a few hours, no harm could come from it. As she said, the city is tightly guarded, and she would not break her vow and try to escape. No, she would not bring down the wrath of the gods on her head, and on her people.

"Go then," he said, "I grant you a few hours. Explain to my sons the journey will be beneficial for them. Counsel them to agree to the plan. Return them to my quarters before sunset, and you prepare to go with your new master."

He turned and walked away, the two guards falling in step behind him. Bah, the Captain thought as he exited from the garden, these Mexicans will never forget their roots. The priests work day and night to show them the true path, and everywhere these ancient gods continue to exist for the natives. Their relationship with the earth and the cosmos is too strong, who knows if we can ever completely stamp out their faith. And she, Malinche, she has that power of the ancients, the powers of the brujos, but Alvarado will tame her spirit.

He laughed aloud, and his laughter echoed in the empty street.

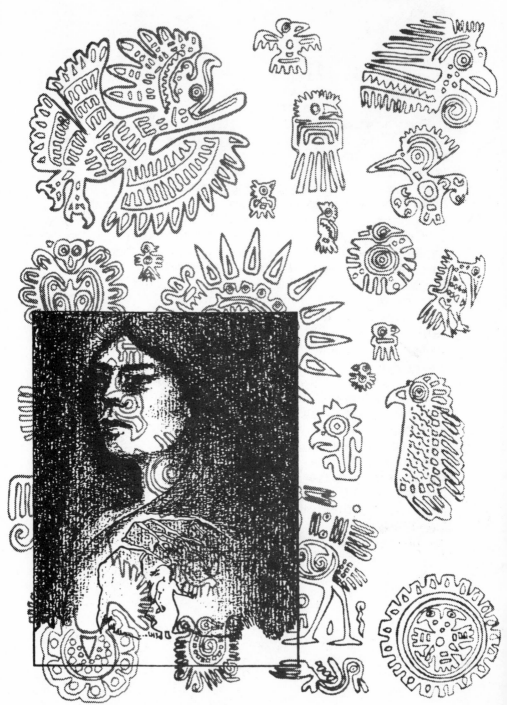

THE SACRIFICE

Malinche cringed when she heard the echo of the Captain's laughter. He had plotted everything so carefully, and he was the victor. Now he had every right to laugh. She had trusted him, and had trusted his love, only to have it lead to bitter betrayal. The end had come, and at this moment she understood why the War God of the Aztecs had given her the vision of sacrifice.

But how could the end be so cruel? She continued to question the vision the War God had given her, even though there was nowhere left to turn for help. The plans of the Captain were complete, and the War God waited for his command to be carried out. The weather seemed to reflect her dilemma, for in the night a storm had come over the city. The sky had been dark all day, and the wind swept through the valley. The War God was angry and waited for his command to be fulfilled.

She would go once more to the temple, she would pray, and she would ask again for guidance.

"Come, my sons," she whispered, "we shall pray at the temple."

75

She led them down the back streets, skirting
the marketplace where the vendors huddled in groups,
discussing the portents of the strange storm and
the fury of the wind which swept across the lake.
There are strange signs in the air, they whispered,
and one by one they closed their stalls, leaving
the marketplace.   It was soon deserted, as silent
as an empty tomb in the heart of the city.

Malinche knocked at the secret entrance and
was admitted by an old priest.   He led the three
to the inner chamber, the Room of the Gods.
Other priests moved in the dark like shadows.
All night and all day they had prayed and burned
incense, asking for guidance.   They knew the
people were uneasy, and there were signs which
had to be interpreted.   But the gods were silent,
the gods had left Mexico-Tenochtitlan.   They
would not speak to the priests, they would not
reveal why the sky grew dark and the volcanos
rumbled with growing energy.   Why did Tlaloc,
the God of Rain, send rain at this unusual time,
rain with wind which destroyed the homes of
the people and caused a turbulence in the lake
which made it flood and wash away the bridges.
Clearly, the gods were displeased, the gods had
deserted the people of Mexico.

The priests turned and watched Malinche as
she entered the chamber with her sons.   They
knew she came to pray to the War God, the strong
warrior Huitzilopochtli.   Perhaps he would speak
to her, perhaps he would tell her what had to
be done to set things right again.   The priests
whispered as they saw Malinche approach the
altar of the War God; a sacrifice would have
to be made.   The priests gathered around Malinche
and her sons while she prayed to the god.   The
answer would come in a vision, and it would
have to be obeyed.

The priest bowed before the War God, he
placed copal on the hot embers of the incense

burner and the fire flared brightly, revealing
the angry visage of Huitzilopochtli. Malinche
lifted her arms and began her incantation, her
prayer to the god.

"God of War," she prayed, "Listen to my prayers.
You who made the Aztecs strong, now make me
strong. Drain me of the love for the man who
now enslaves my people. Remove this tyrant from
my heart. I followed his footsteps once, I bore
him sons, but the prophecy of my destiny has become
a lie. Peace has not come, our future is not
secure, slavery has a new name...."

She prayed and revealed her soul to the God
of War, and the dark chamber grew suffocating
with the sweet smoke of incense. She prayed with
urgency in her words, realizing that if the god
repeated the vision he had once given her, as
horrible as it might be, she had to carry out his
will. And as she prayed her heart grew cold, the
love she once knew died. Now she could be as
cold and cruel as those who made war.

"Make me strong!" she cried. "Blind my
eyes to the blood I must shed! As I was once
the first consort of the Spaniard, now make
me a warrior against his enslavement! I pray,
tell me what I must do! Mexico must be free!
Must my own sons be the first warriors to die in
this struggle? Must they lead the way for the
future, for the reign of Quetzalcoatl?"

As before, she heard the god answer her
prayers. Yes, the voice in the interior of the
chamber seemed to say, the spirits of your sons
will guide the warriors of the new struggle. A
new breed of men born of this world will come behind them to free Mexico, to free the spirit of the
people. Mexico will be free! And you, Malinche,
will live forever in the legends of your people.
Go now, spill the blood of the warriors! The
blood will cleanse you of the past, Mexico will
enter a new age! Go!

The God of War thundered the last command. Malinche cried out in terror and fell to the ground, sobbing with dread and pain. At her heart she felt the knife she carried, the ancient knife of the Aztec priests. When she rose to her feet she saw her sons and the gathered priests. Had they too seen the vision and heard the commands of the god?

"It is time to go," the priest whispered as he leaned down and took her hand. "Be strong, obey the commands of the gods. They are the spirits of our ancient ancestors, they know how to cure the fear and enslavement we suffer. Do not think that this is the end of life, it is but the beginning of a new cycle of time. The ancient prophecies were correct, the end of one era has come, the lake will be replenished with the blood of our warriors, their spirits shall live forever. Do not be afraid."

Malinche rose and nodded. What he said was true. Her sons would live forever, the waters of the lake would be charged with new energy, just as ancient sacrifices had renewed the sun. The people were entering a new era, and death was but a stepping stone. What seemed so cruel in the god's command would pass with time. Her sons would be remembered forever. Now she had to put away the past and think of her commitment to the future, to the freedom of her people. She had to be strong.

"Come," the priest said. "You will have to go through the tunnel which leads to the shore of the lake. The entrance you used to enter here is now sealed. The soldiers are searching the marketplace, they are everywhere."

He led Malinche and her sons to a secret door, a huge stone door which the other priests opened for them to pass. "This will lead to the sacred place," the priest instructed, "there where our first ancestors found the eagle on the nopal, there where the golden fish swim in the pond."

Malinche thanked him.   She looked at her sons.
What had they seen?   What did they know?   If they
sensed anything they did not show it.   They stood
straight, ready to follow her.   Then she realized,
they too had prayed while they waited, they too
had asked to share in the vision of the future.
Her sons were warriors ready to go forward: one
a warrior of Huitzilopochtli the War God, strong
and resolute in understanding his role in the
struggle for freedom, the other, a follower of
Quetzalcoatl, a follower of the path of light
and knowledge, and together they were the two
parts of the new man, the new man of Mexico. They
would live forever.   This was but the first step
in their long destiny.   Others would come after
them, the crest would grow, Mexico would be free.
   "Ready, my sons?"
   "We are ready," they replied.   They entered
the passageway and heard the stone door close
after them.   Slowly they made their way through
the winding tunnel, praying as they went, knowing
the exit was by the edge of the lake where they
had spent so much of their time contemplating
the waters of the quiet lake, learning the stories
of the golden fish which swam in the waters of
the pond.
   A howling wind met them as they emerged from
the mouth of the tunnel, a wind which churned
the waters of the angry lake.   Dry lightning
flashed in the sultry sky.   The world seemed deserted, only the three figures stood illuminated
in the eerie light of the setting sun and the
flashes of lightning.
   Malinche looked at the angry waters.   The
tempest around her reflected the anger of the
people, it reflected the end of time.   In all of
Mexico only one person could set it right, only
one person had heard the voice of the gods.   She,
Malinche, again saw the image of the obsidian
knife, and she heard the words of the God of War.

Mexico would be free! Many would die, but others
would come behind them to prepare the way for the
god of peace, Quetzalcoatl!

Then she heard another cry, the far off calls
of the soldiers. Had she been discovered? She
had to act quickly. She took the dark knife from
its sheath and held it to the sky. Lightning
flashed and glinted off the shiny stone. She
looked at her sons. For a moment her resolve left
her and she felt weak and empty. But the boys
did not move, they looked at her as if they understood what had to be done, like warriors who do
not fear death. Malinche understood, and this
filled her with an inner peace.

But again the shouts of the soldiers sounded,
and in the dusk she saw the torches of approaching
men.

LA LLORONA

In his quarters the Captain paced nervously. He was angry with himself for allowing Malinche to have time alone to speak to the boys. Within the hour he had returned to the garden, but they were not there. He had sent out guards to search the city; he had searched her sleeping quarters, but there was no trace of her or his sons. He cursed silently as he blamed himself for agreeing with Malinche's request.

Where could she be, he asked himself. He had been assured by the guards at the bridges that she had not crossed. Could she have taken a canoe and crossed the lake? But where would she go? His spies were everywhere, and none had reported seeing her. She had disappeared as if into thin air. Did she have the power to fly? During his time in Mexico he had heard of brujos and shamans who could fly. The people believed in that power, and Malinche had studied with many of those men of wisdom. He had seen what she could do with fire, it seemed to obey her will. She had caused blinding flashes of fire to flare up in the face

of the enemy. But no, he shook his head. He was
just nervous. Of course she couldn't fly! Neither
man nor woman could fly, that claim was made only
by witches!

She would return, she had given her vow. She
had said she would part with her sons, and she had
sworn by the gods of her ancestors. Such a vow
had to be kept, or else, the natives believed, the
gods would strike the person dead, and the soul
would be doomed to wander without rest throughout
eternity. That judgement they feared more than
any other.

Now the wind and rain lashed the city. The
afternoon had become almost as dark as night with
the sun deeply overcast. Outside only the sudden
and terrible flashes of lightning provided light
by which to see. The Captain moved to the door
and donned his cloak. There was no point in
waiting, he would go out and join in the search
himself. A knock at the door interrupted him.

He threw the door open and the Princess hurried
in, wet and trembling from the storm.

"Isabela? What are you doing out in the
storm? Come in, warm yourself." He took her
cape and offered her a dry blanket.

"I grew worried," the Princess answered.
Her face was drawn and pale. "When the storm
began to rage my servants all huddled in fear,
talking in whispers. I demanded to know what
they were saying. They told me it was the end
of the world. The rain will fill the lake and
destroy the city, they said, the mountains will
explode with fire and end everything. When the
storm worsened, they disappeared."

"Disappeared?" the Captain asked. "What do
you mean?"

"After I left you, I went to my quarters to
prepare for my journey. When I called for my
servants I discovered they were all gone. Just
like that, the entire place was empty. When I

went out I found the entire city deserted. The people have left. The marketplace is empty."

"Yes," the Captain acknowledged, "the guards have reported this. I do not like it, trouble is brewing...."

"The end of the world," the shivering Princess repeated to herself, "and all men and women shall be made beasts, they said."

"Calm yourself," the Captain said. "Those are only stories. There is no truth in them. But there is a mystery, Malinche is missing."

"What?" the Princess exclaimed.

"She has not returned," the Captain nodded. "Even now I have all my guards searching for her."

"I do not trust that woman," the Princess cried and wrung her hands. "She will destroy us if she has the chance."

"We must find her, find my sons," the Captain answered.

"Forget her!" the Princess exclaimed. "Let's save ourselves. Order an escort to take us out of the city! We can reach the ship in a few days and set sail without any of them!"

"I cannot leave," the Captain said, surprised at the insistence of the Princess. "I am the Captain General. Mexico is my kingdom. If I leave, it will only be to attend His Majesty and comply with his wishes. But even then I must go with my sons. You said he expressly said I was to return with my sons."

"I lied," the Princess blurted out. "I lied to trick you to return. I knew taking them and presenting them at court would be very important to you. It was for you...."

"You lied!" the Captain said in astonishment.

"Yes," the Princess sobbed. "I lied because I wanted you to return to Spain. Once there I knew you would see how important you are to the court! You would be rewarded! You would live a civilized life, not like here in this heathen country where life is such a daily struggle! Oh, how I have grown to hate it. Yes, I lied, but I had your welfare in mind."

The Captain shook his head. Suddenly he realized the great mistake he had made. Malinche had been right, she had told the truth, and he had rewarded her with threats and banishment. What a fool he had been. No, Spain would never reward him, they had no need for him, the conqueror of the New World. They were only pleased to receive the gold he sent. His home was here in Mexico, his sons were Mexicans, not Spaniards. But even here he would never be honored, he would always be the conqueror, the man of iron who rode on horseback and brought much destruction. That's how the natives knew him.

"You've grown quiet, what are you thinking?" the Princess asked.

"I'm thinking something may be saved from all this," he said and reached for the door.

"Where are you going?" she asked.

"We are going to find Malinche," he said and grabbed her wrist, dragging her out into the storm with him, "and hope it is not too late!"

"No!" she shouted. "It's madness! She is insane! Why endanger our lives looking for her?"

"Because she has my sons with her!" the Captain responded harshly.

"But you don't know where to search!"

"She has a favorite place by the edge of the lake," the Captain shouted above the roar of the wind. "We will go there!"

"There is evil in the storm, my Lord."

"No more evil than we do!" answered the Captain. He dragged the unwilling Princess through the dark, praying as they went that he would find Malinche and his sons at that pond by the lake where the golden fish swam. There was no other place to search. Still, as he pulled the reluctant Princess towards the lake he was filled with apprehension. What would they find? And why did the cry of the wind carry in it the sound of grief, as of a woman crying in mourning? Were the women of Mexico–Tenochtitlan grieving the end of the world?

Around them the lightning brightened the sky as it flashed in jagged bursts over the land, and the thunder shook the earth. In the distance, around the mountainous rim of the city, he could see flashes of volcanos which lit the distant sky.

"Please, my Lord," the Princess begged. "We will never find them in this storm! Let us return to safety! This is madness!" The wind tore at her cloak and hair. She had never seen a storm which raged with such fury, and she was truly afraid.

"We must find her!" the Captain shouted above the wind. They pushed ahead, fighting the horrendous wind, until they neared the edge of the lake. In the lightning's flash they could see the great causeways and bridges which had been torn away by the fury of the storm. The furious waves of the lake pounded against the shore, adding their roar to the sound of the storm. Never had the Captain seen the lake so violent and deadly. The elements were indeed out of kilter, their power no longer benign but totally destructive.

The shore of the lake was deserted, lit only by the continuing lightning bolts. They struggled on until the Princess cried out and pointed to a group of lights which came towards them. She uttered a prayer and made the sign of the cross because she believed the demons of the dreadful storm were upon them.

"Dear Lord, what is it?" she asked. The flaring lights drew closer.

"Halt!" the Captain shouted. "Who goes there? Man or demon, I command you to stop!"

"My Captain General," a voice came back. "It is I, Alvarado!" He and two soldiers drew near, the lights were torches they carried, fires whipped by the wind to create eerie patterns in the darkness. In the torchlight the Captain saw Alvarado's face; it was grotesque with shock and fear.

"We have seen her! We have seen her!" Alvarado cried and clutched at the Captain.

"Oh, my dear God in heaven," one of the soldiers moaned and dropped to his knees. He covered his face with his hands and wept. The second soldier did not speak, but terror was written on his face. They had seen ghosts, or the devil himself, for their voices quaked with fear.

"Tell me, where have you seen Malinche?" the Captain shouted. He looked into the faces of the men, his soldiers who had been through many campaigns of war with him. He had never seen them in such shock. A cold fear ran through his body. Alvarado's voice broke as he answered.

"We have seen Malinche...even now she comes up the shore of the lake...crying for her children...."

Even as he said this, a piercing cry split the air, rising above the sound of the wind. It was the cry of a woman in great anguish.

"That is Malinche!" Alvarado cried.

"The demon woman," a soldier added, and he made the sign of the cross to ward off the evil.

"I see no one," the Captain said. "Tell me what happened?"

"I beg you, my Captain," Alvarado answered, trying to compose himself. "Do not ask me to report what I have seen tonight."

"But you say you saw Malinche," the Captain demanded.

"We saw a woman, or a witch, run along the edge of the lake, a bloodied knife in her hand..." the soldier on his knees muttered. He spoke to himself, as if whatever he had seen had driven him mad.

Again the wailing sound of the crying woman filled the air.

"My dear God," the Princess whispered and drew closer to the Captain. She had never heard such a frightening sound, but she knew it was the cry of a woman in grief, a cry which rose like pain from the soul.

"Malinche," the Captain whispered her name. Again he peered into the dark but could see nothing. He felt the hair along his neck rise.

"She's there, following us," one soldier said. "She's there in the dark, waiting for us...."

"Tell me what you saw," the Captain commanded again, although he dreaded what he might hear.

"We searched as you commanded," Alvarado said. "We came along the edge of the lake. Suddenly we saw her, standing there with her sons. We called to her, not knowing if we had found her or some demon of the storm. She saw us, and she commanded us to stop, and I swear, my Captain, we could not move. Then we saw her raise the knife...it shimmered in the flashes of the lightning. She held it high, as if she were a priestess in a ceremony of sacrifice, and the boys did not move, they did not scream. Dear God, please, ask me to say no more!"

"Speak!" the Captain ordered.

"She murdered the children," Alvarado sobbed. "She murdered the children. As God is my witness, we saw her murder the innocent children, your sons...."

The Captain cried out and clutched at his heart. Never in battle had he felt such fear or weakness. His strength left him.

"No! You are lying! It is not true...."

"It is true, my Lord," Alvarado continued, compelled now to tell the story to its end. "When we saw her do this terrible deed we could not move. Then quickly as the murder was done she picked up the bodies of those two innocent victims and cast them into the burning lake...yes, the lake seemed to be burning with fire in its rage. The waves reached out like death's fingers and received the children, and then, my Captain, the lake grew still."

The Princess moaned, faint with fear she dropped to her knees. She had played a part in the events which led to this dreadful murder, now she felt the same anguish which had filled Malinche. This was the most hideous crime of womanhood, the unforgivable crime of a mother, the unspoken terror. Yes, if this was true then indeed the world had lost its reason and was coming to an end. She sobbed uncontrollably, aware of her insignificance in the face of such terror and horror.

"Oh God in heaven," the Captain declared, "forgive us for the things we have done to draw Your wrath upon our heads. For if what we hear is true, then we are the guilty ones!"

Then again the piercing cry of Malinche was heard, this time nearer. A shadow emerged from the dark, a cry split the air and echoed in the dark.

"Malinche," the Captain called. "Show yourself! Have no fear of us, for it is we who must ask your forgiveness!"

"There!" One of the soldiers pointed.

The shadow drew closer, a lightning flash revealed Malinche, her white gown covered with blood, her long hair flowing in the wind. In one hand she still carried the bloody dagger of sacrifice.

"My children! My children!" she sobbed. "The gods have taken my children from me and cast them in the lake. Oh dark waters of the lake, I pray you return my children to me."

Her cry of pain and anguish rose in the air and became a part of the wail of the howling wind. The group in front of her fell to their knees and prayed for forgiveness.

"Malinche," the Captain whispered her name softly. "Our wrongs have led you to this terrible deed. Our wrongs are beyond all human understanding."

"Yes, I have been wronged," Malinche answered, standing tall and noble before them. "My sons were to be made slaves, and I paid for their liberation dearly. Now they are dead...but other sons of Mexico will rise against you and avenge this deed. The future will not forgive any of us."

"God have mercy on our souls," answered the Captain.

"Listen," Malinche responded. "Do you hear the cry of my sons? They cry in the waters of the lake. They call for me to come. I go now, transformed by this deed into the eternal mother who cannot sleep until she finds her sons. I will never tire of that search, not until all of my sons are safe in my arms. I, Malinche, princess and mother of the Mexicans, will forever be known as the woman who cries for her sons...."

She turned and disappeared into the dark. For her deed that night, she left behind her grief and penance, and her wailing cry.

Credits

THE LEGEND OF LA LLORONA

Drawings

by

DESOLINA

Mexican Indian bird motifs

Book layout and design

by

OCTAVIO I. ROMANO-V

Other **Tonatiuh–Quinto Sol** books

by

Rudolfo A. Anaya

———

BLESS ME, ULTIMA   Novel

THE SILENCE OF THE LLANO   Short stories

———